OPTIMISTIC
PEACEFUL
RELAXED
TRUSTFUL
CALM
CHEERFUL
HAPPY
WOW! LOOK AT ALL THESE POSITIVE FEELINGS!
KIND
ENTHUSIASTIC
LOVE
JOY
PLAYFUL
CARING

My FEEL GOOD BOOK

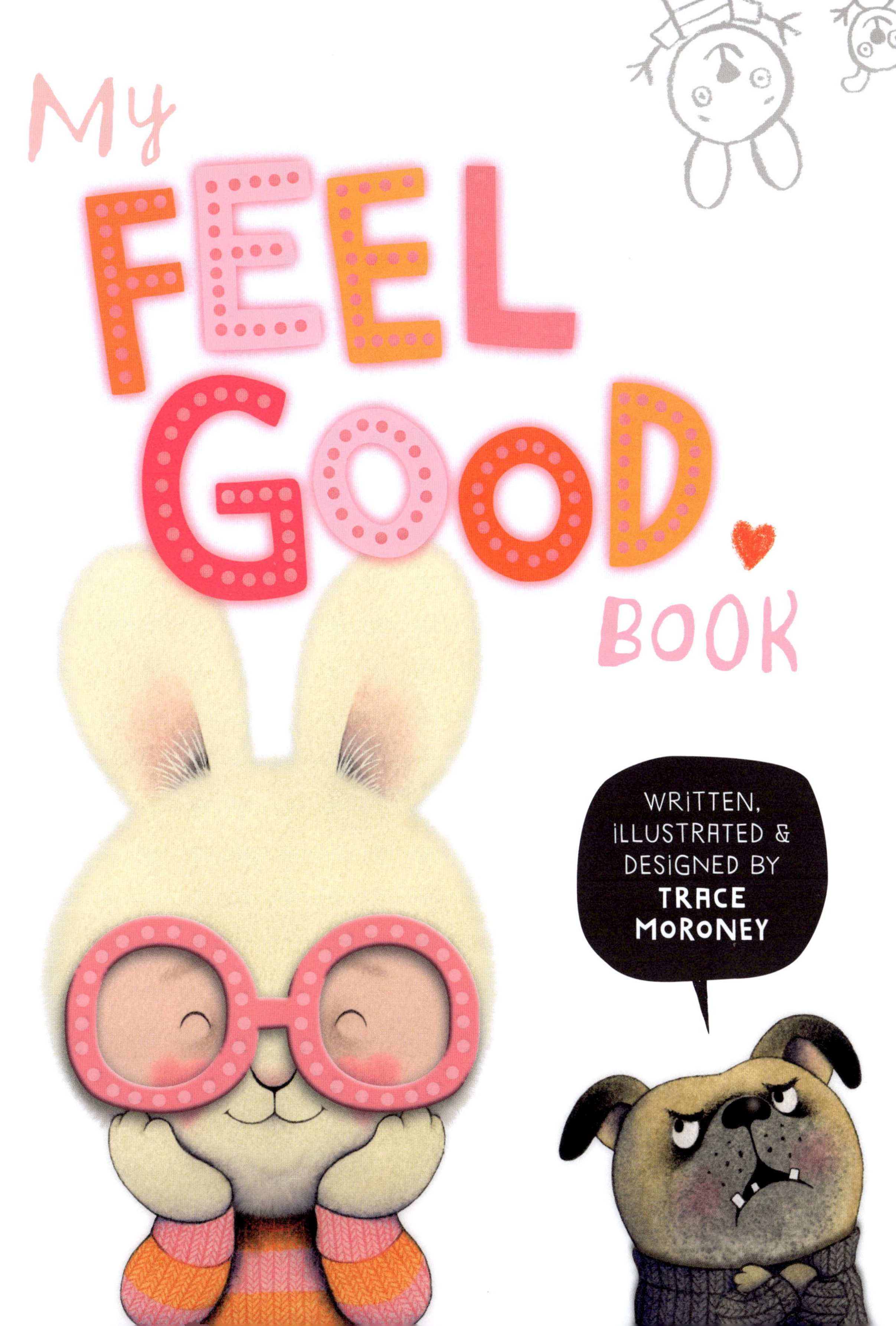

POSITIVE THINKING

is when you think about the good things in your life **more often** than you think about the not-so-good things.

And ... it's when you think about yourself and the things you do in a healthy, balanced, and positive way.

HUMPH!
IT CAN'T BE THAT EASY!

A **POSITIVE MINDSET** is when positive thinking is a **habit** ... and you tend to focus on the bright side, expect good things to happen, and deal with challenges or problems with a positive attitude ... and an **open mind**!

Having a positive mindset is like looking through
rose-coloured glasses ... and seeing the world
in a positive, cheerful, and rosy light!

OOOOO ... THAT LOOKS LOVELY! IMAGINE IF EVERYONE IN THE WHOLE WIDE WORLD WORE ROSE-COLOURED GLASSES.

But ... having a positive mindset doesn't always mean simply smiling, being cheerful, or bursting with happiness all the time!

And it doesn't mean ignoring or avoiding bad things ... or that you won't have uncomfortable or difficult feelings.

Having a positive mindset means understanding you won't always be happy, accepting difficult feelings or challenges when they come, making the best out of any situation you find yourself in, and ... seeing yourself and the things you do in a positive light.

UH-OH ...
THERE'S A
FEELINGS STORM
COMING!

It's important not to hide behind your rose-coloured glasses, or pretend to be happy or positive ... especially if it's not how you're really feeling.

And ... thinking or saying positive things all the time is not always helpful ... sometimes it can be hurtful. Like when someone tells you (or you tell yourself) to:

... especially when you're struggling to cope with something really, **really** hard or feeling down.

While most people say this
positive stuff to help you feel better,
it can actually make you feel worse ...
because it can feel like they are
ignoring your feelings ... and that
you – and your feelings – **JUST**

DON'T

MATTER

Remember, it's not normal to feel happy all the time, *in fact* ... it's impossible!

But ... having a positive mindset **is** something you can have all the time – which makes it easier to cope with the hard stuff when it happens.

FEELINGS STORMS

PROBLEMS AND SETBACKS

DIFFICULT AND UNCOMFORTABLE FEELINGS

HARD STUFF

A positive mindset is something you can grow and nurture (take care of) every day for the rest of your life ... starting right now!

To grow a happier and more positive you, it's important to learn and practise these things:

THESE ARE TRICKY WORDS TO UNDERSTAND SO ASK FOR HELP IF YOU NEED IT.

1

RESILIENCE
(how to say it: **re-zil-i-enss**):
Being able to adapt or bounce back from disappointment, challenges, and failure. And understanding that when you make a mistake or something bad happens, you can learn and grow from it.

2
GRATITUDE
(how to say it: grat-i-tyood):
Feeling and being thankful for the good things in your life ... and the lessons learned from the not-so-good things.
THANK YOU FOR BEING KIND, THANK YOU FOR BEING MY GOOD FRIEND, AND THANK YOU FOR BEING YOU!

3

ACCEPTANCE

(how to say it: **ak-sep-tanss**):
Knowing things don't always go the way you want them to; you won't always be happy; and understanding that hard stuff and uncomfortable feelings are a part of life.

4

iNTEGRiTY

(how to say it: **in-teg-ri-tee**):
Being honest, 'real', and doing the 'right thing' ... even when no-one is looking!

5

MINDFULNESS

(how to say it: **mind-ful-ness**):
Being totally focused and aware of things at every moment ... like what you are doing; your breathing; how your body feels; and what you can hear, see, and feel – without being distracted by thoughts about the past or the future. Be in the moment!

6

OPTIMISM

(how to say it: **op-ti-mizz-im**):
Feeling hopeful about things in the future, or expecting a good outcome for something you are about to do.

Here are some things you can do to **supercharge** your positive mindset, and to make you feel really good about being **YOU**:

LEARN AND GROW

Think about your past problems and setbacks as a chance to learn and grow. **Everyone** has problems and setbacks, but it's being able to pick yourself up, adapt, and move on from them that matters. Ask yourself what you have learned, what you would do differently in the future, and what positive things have happened (if any) because of the setback.

SEARCH FOR THE GOOD STUFF

Think about the things you are good at and love to do, and find ways to do more of these things throughout each day. **Have fun, be funny, laugh,** and focus on the good things – no matter how small they are.

START EACH DAY WITH A POSITIVE THOUGHT

Keep a jar full of positive words and sayings beside your bed. When you wake up, reach into the jar and read something that makes you feel good about you and the day ahead!

POSITIVE WORDS

Use positive words to describe yourself. Change saying or thinking "I am stupid" to "I am finding this hard to learn, but I am going to do my best", or "I can't" to "I'm going to give this a go." Try to use positive words more often, as this helps to train your brain into thinking in a more positive way.

BE KIND
Be kind to yourself and others ... even to someone you don't know. Help an elderly neighbour with a chore, or help a friend with some school work, or be there to listen and support them when they are struggling with a problem.
PRACTISE MINDFULNESS
Focus on what's happening with you and for you right now – in every moment – instead of worrying about what has happened in the past ... or what may or may not happen in the future.

POSITIVE PEEPS

Spend more time with positive people – like friends, family members, coaches, or others who support and encourage you.

SET GOALS

Set goals (things you would like to do or achieve), and plan the things you need to do to reach each goal.
Break each goal down into mini-goals or steps. Share them with your positive peeps, and ask for help if you need it.

ACCEPT WHAT HAPPENS

Accept what happens, even when it's not what you wanted ... including having a good time if you are not doing as well as you hoped!
Learn to accept and manage difficult feelings or challenges when they come.

goals

KEEP A 'FEEL GOOD' JOURNAL

Every night, before you go to sleep, write down three good things (or best moments) that happened that day, and one thing you are looking forward to tomorrow. After doing this for a while, you will notice more and more positive things to be thankful for ... including more positive thoughts and feelings!

THREE GOOD THINGS that happened today:

1. I ate some broccoli AND I liked it!
2. I helped a neighbour tidy their garden.
3. I went on a bike ride with Mum.

TOMORROW: I AM LOOKING FORWARD TO: Having a picnic at the park and playing with my friends.

BEING THANKFUL IS THE MOST POWERFUL WAY TO MAKE POSITIVE FEELINGS LAST LONGER!

FEEL
OOD

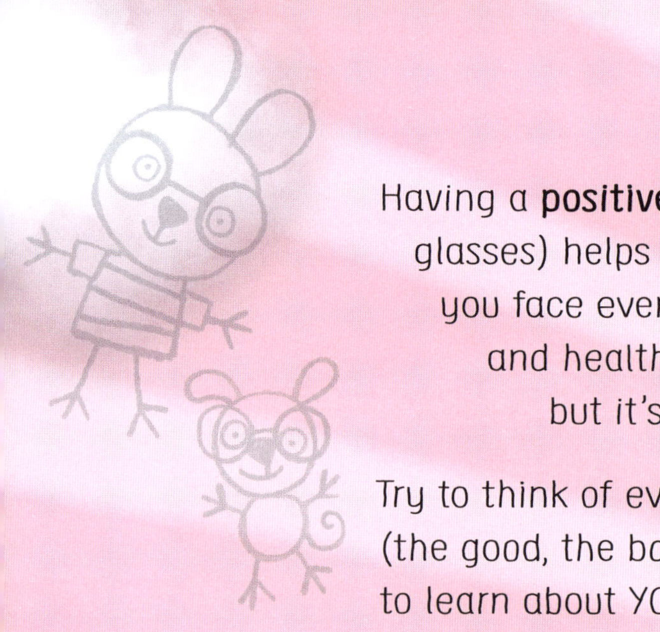

Having a **positive mindset** (or wearing rose-coloured glasses) helps you cope with the ups and downs you face every day, and helps you be happier and healthier and open to new things ... but it's important to keep it real!

Try to think of every experience, thought, and feeling (the good, the bad, and the in-between) as a chance to learn about YOU ... like the things you are good at, the things you are not so good at (laugh about these), and remember ... your positive mindset is your

SUPERPOWER!

WOOOHOOO! THIS POSITIVE THINKING THING SURE DOES MAKE ME FEEL GOOD!

THREE GOOD THINGS

A FEEL GOOD ACTIVITY

This is an awesome activity to boost your feelings of happiness, gratitude, and overall wellbeing by writing down and savouring good or funny things that happened in your day.

Savouring means letting the good memories and feelings hang around for longer.

Do these three steps every night before you go to sleep:

Remember three good things that happened today.
Think about the three good things you saw, heard, or did – and let the memories take over your mind. Notice the positive feelings that come along with them.

Write down the three good things.
Write down the three good things that happened today. Use as many or as few words as you like – and don't worry about perfect spelling or grammar – this is meant to be fun and capture your positive feelings!

Think about why these three things happened.
Write down why each of these good things happened, what or who helped make them good, and if or how you were involved in them.

After a week or two of doing this every day, feelings of happiness grow and can last for six months. WOW! ... that's half of a whole year!

PHOTOCOPY THIS PAGE OR SCAN THIS QR CODE OR GO TO WWW.TRACEMORONEY.COM OR MAKE YOUR OWN.

My THREE GOOD THINGS

1

2

3

DATE:

NOTES TO PARENTS AND CAREGIVERS

Most of us know someone who has a buoyant and happy energy, and find ourselves drawn to them in the hope that it is infectious! And, indeed, it is! More importantly, how do we help our children cultivate and nurture a more positive attitude about themselves and the world around them?

What is a positive mindset?
A positive mindset is the general tendency to focus on the good in life, expect positive outcomes, and approach challenges or difficulties with a positive and balanced outlook. A positive mindset is when positive thinking becomes a habit – in other words, with effort and practice, you start to think more positively in a way that feels natural and authentic, and you create a lens from which you view your world in a kinder, 'rosier' way.

Having a positive mindset doesn't mean avoiding or ignoring negative feelings, or that you won't experience adversity; instead, it involves searching for the silver lining, making the best out of any situation, and seeing difficult experiences as an opportunity for growth.

Increasing positive thoughts and emotions opens up our minds to opportunities and possibilities, broadens and builds resources and coping skills, improves our overall psychological and physical health and wellbeing, promotes resilience, and helps reduce the harmful effects of negative emotions.

What is toxic (or false) positivity?
Toxic positivity is the expectation to be happy and positive, despite how dire or emotionally difficult a situation is, and disregards negative emotions. Some signs of toxic positivity are ignoring your problems and negative feelings; feeling guilty for being upset, sad, or angry; telling yourself or others phrases like 'be happy' or 'just stay positive' in response to a difficult situation; hiding uncomfortable or painful feelings; and dismissing – or not acknowledging – others' difficult feelings.

Our human brains are wired to dwell more on negative thoughts and experiences than positive ones, but with a positive mindset we are better equipped to cope with the hard stuff when it happens and respond with optimism, resilience, and gratitude.

Here are some ways to help your child develop a positive mindset:

- Together with your child, learn about and discuss the key components of a positive mindset: resilience, gratitude, integrity, optimism, acceptance, and mindfulness. Share simple ways you have expressed and practised these attributes every day.

Acknowledge your child's feelings. Try not to dismiss their negative feelings by telling them to 'cheer up' or have 'happy vibes only'. Instead, ***be*** a soft and safe place for your child to share their concerns or feel comfortable asking you for help. Don't forget to acknowledge their positive feelings too!

Model positive thinking. Your child will learn to model the behaviours they observe in you, including how you react and respond to both negative and positive experiences.
Be mindful of how you talk about yourself (and others), and transform negative self-talk into positive self-talk.

Healthy living. Try to ensure your child has a healthy and balanced diet, drinks lots of water, exercises daily, and gets enough restful and restorative sleep. Being sleep-deprived or consuming toxic substances – such as an overload of sugar – can greatly interfere with our body's ability to function optimally ... including regulating thoughts, moods, and emotions.

At bedtime, ask your child what the best moments of their day were – and share yours with them. This creates a warm, loving, and positive state of mind, which helps to promote restful sleep.

Write loving, supportive notes to your child to discover at the beginning of each day, or pop it in their school bag or lunch box. Positive affirmations can help set the intention for a good day!

Encourage your child to set goals. Have them plan the steps they need to take to reach each goal – and celebrate the accomplishment of each step. Discuss potential obstacles that may pop up along the way and prepare coping strategies in the event they happen, and let them know you are there to help and support them. While achieving the goal may be important, encourage your child to focus on – and enjoy – the ***process*** (or journey).

The secret to happiness is gratitude! Encourage your child to focus on the positive aspects of life and make it a daily practice to identify and appreciate what they already have in this very moment, for example, 'I am thankful for ...' or 'I am grateful that ...'.
While positive emotions about things or events wear off quickly, feeling deep appreciation – or gratitude – makes feelings of happiness long-lasting.
So get good at practising gratitude and notice your happiness grow!

For more information and support material visit: www.tracemoroney.com

Happiness is when what you think,
what you say, and what you do
are in harmony.

Mahatma Gandhi

Published with love by EQ Publications Ltd
www.eqpublications.nz

www.tracemoroney.com
Edited by Madeleine Collinge

Printed in China by
RR Donnelley Asia Printing Solutions Ltd.

First published 2024.